MASQUERADE

A PRIDE & PREJUDICE SENSUAL INTIMATE VARIATION

CORA ASTON

Edited by
MISS EDITRIX

LONGBOURN LIBRARY

She took a deep breath, steadying her pounding heart. "I fear I may have given you the wrong impression, Sir, and I realize now I must refuse to attend the ball."

He stilled, watching her with the unblinking intensity of a hunter. She moved away a step, attempting to break the draw of his body, so near her own.

"I do not have the sophistication to indulge in a flirtation of the kind I am told the worldly ladies and gentlemen of London often do, and I cannot allow you to believe I would ever . . ." Her voice faltered, because she knew once she denied him forever, she would never see him again. But so be it. "I cannot be your mistress. I am not saying that is what you had in mind, or even that you would deign to ask, but I am a simple woman and unversed in these sorts of games. I do not know how to judge your behavior."

She firmed her mouth to avoid allowing him to see her tremble as she looked away. Humiliation curled in her breast, for she had admitted her ignorance as well as, perhaps, made a laughable presumption.

"Is that why you believe I want, Elizabeth?" he asked, voice soft. "To have you as my mistress?"

She said nothing. What could she say? She had already laid herself bare. At least she had not suffered the ultimate indignation and admitted her love for him only to have him scorn her. At least that final secret she might keep hidden in her heart.

"I do not want you for my mistress," he said. "Here."

Confused, she glanced at him, staring at the box he held out. "I do not understand."

"I expect to see you at the ball tonight, Elizabeth. If I do not, I will be forced to fetch you, and then I will be in a poor mood."

JOIN THE NEWSLETTER

New Release announcements,
giveaways,
ARC opportunities,
flash sales.

smarturl.it/coraaston

JOIN

CHAPTER 1

Elizabeth attempted to ignore the knot in her middle as they drove up the lane of Pemberley Park. I should not have come, she thought. I should have pled some illness and stayed behind and allowed my aunt and uncle the pleasure without me.

The knowledge that she had misjudged Mr. Darcy weighed on Elizabeth's mind. She had arrogantly thought her opinion of him to be final, as if no man was capable of change and she incapable of misunderstanding. She wrestled with herself, with the conflicting desire to both avoid him and to offer him an apology as well as gratitude for his part in reuniting Jane with Mr. Bingley.

"The most astonishing thing has occurred, Lizzy," Jane had said months ago. "I have received a letter from Mr. Darcy, and you would not credit the confession it contains."

A confession followed by a call from Mr. Bingley, explaining he had also received such a letter and that Mr. Darcy had admitted to regrettable interference in their courtship, and urged Bingley to renew his sentiments to the lady, for Mr. Darcy believed his suit would be most welcome.

Jane and Charles wed by special license not a week later, choosing an intimate ceremony and small family breakfast for their celebration. Mr. Darcy had been unable to attend due to an illness in the family, but wished the couple sincere happiness. It was then Elizabeth had truly begun to realize that though Darcy had made a mistake, so had she. Only she could not correct hers by simply sending a letter. If she did, it could be misconstrued as an attempt to earn her way back into his affections, and she knew better. Mr. Darcy's good opinion, after all, once lost was lost forever.

She took some small comfort in the beauty and elegance of the grounds of Pemberley. A masterful eye was in charge, she could tell, for nature had been allowed to take its course without tasteless interference from man.

"When he marries," her aunt murmured, "his wife will surely be happy to be mistress of all this."

Elizabeth smiled weakly. The mistress might, through some quirk of fate were she a less stubborn and tempestuous person, have been her. She would never admit it, however, not only because it would appear to be bragging, but because of her sense of humiliation over her behavior. And if she admitted to the proposal and her refusal, she would be obliged to tell the entire tale.

She had learned her lesson. Her lips were sealed forever.

The housekeeper admitted Elizabeth and the Gardiners to the grand home, seeming to take pride in escorting them through the public areas until they came to the gallery.

"Such a handsome estate," her uncle exclaimed. "So well-appointed. And the master is not often at home?"

"I daresay more than most masters," the housekeeper, Mrs. Reynolds, replied. "Though I would wish he was home more often. Tomorrow we shall have the pleasure of his company once more, however."

Elizabeth faltered for a half step, then forced herself to continue walking.

"Ah!" her aunt said. "That is why I detected such happy bustle about the house."

Mrs. Reynolds smiled and lowered her voice as if imparting a confidence. "He is to bring a large party of friends with him and has given the order to prepare for a ball. That is why there is more activity than usual, we must ensure Master Darcy finds no fault in our preparations."

"Your attention to duty does you and your master much credit," her aunt replied. As they toured the room, a small portrait took Mrs. Gardiner's attention. "Elizabeth! Look, I believe it is Mr. Wickham."

"Indeed it is," the housekeeper said, eyebrow rising. "You are acquainted?"

Elizabeth drew closer out of morbid curiosity, though gazing upon even a still likeness of him made her stomach curdle. She had nearly been taken in by his charming, deceitful countenance, only to learn he had thrown over their burgeoning understanding for a lady with greater prospects. Then to learn of his dastardly behavior with Mr. Darcy's sister, of an age with her own. The urge to protect and avenge a beloved sister, Elizabeth well understood. She also understood being forced to disclose such an incident in a letter in order to clear his own name would have infuriated Mr. Darcy.

How foolish she had been, so rash to rush to Wickham's defense and refuse Mr. Darcy, only to then learn the truth. Only to then realize that her feelings ran deeper and were more complicated than she had first supposed. She might have been Mrs. Darcy. She might have been his beloved wife.

"My niece is acquainted," her aunt was saying. "And I believe she also made the acquaintance of Mr. Darcy while he spent some time near her home."

The housekeeper seemed surprised, then looked upon Elizabeth with a small measure more of respect. Not that her manners had been unpleasant before but there was a new gravity in the woman's eyes, as if Elizabeth was now worthy of more honor simply by knowing Mr. Darcy.

"I know him a little," Elizabeth said. "I cannot claim any great friendship."

"And did you not find him to be an affable, handsome man, miss?"

What could she say to that inquiry? Yes, of course, though the truth was so much more complicated. "Yes, very handsome."

Mrs. Reynolds led them to another portrait, and Elizabeth stared, breath caught. His eyes looked directly at her, clear and frank, his bearing dignified without the air of coldness he had shown from the beginning at Meryton.

"This is he, Aunt," Elizabeth said. "Mr. Darcy."

"Well! He is, indeed, a fine looking fellow. And he has a sister, I recall?"

"Oh, yes," Mrs. Reynolds said. "An accomplished, lovely young lady she is, too. Such a gentle disposition. Mr. Darcy adores her and with good cause. He would do anything to make her happy."

"A veritable St. George," Elizabeth muttered, then winced, imagining herself as the dragon at the wrong end of Mr. Darcy's very sharp sword.

She listened with discomfort through the tour of the house as the housekeeper sang her master's praises. Indeed, as they passed servants clad in somber but elegant livery, going about their work with a cheerful countenance, Elizabeth grew to realize that her understanding of Mr. Darcy's character was not only limited but likely very wrong. But then, she had already accepted her wrong in believing him unpleasant and disdainful. His letter, while formal, had been that of a man laying bare his heart. He could have lashed out but he had not. Instead, he had demonstrated a kind of quiet, dignified humility. Elizabeth simply had not realized how deep her ignorance ran.

Had she truly expected a man of his consequence to be like Mr. Bingley? Effusive, open, warm as a sunny day? No, Mr. Darcy's feelings ran as deep as an underground lake, the surface still and mysterious. Was not that sort of quiet dignity to be preferred? She had often thought Mr. Bingley's chatter would drive her to distraction if she were his wife, though Jane's gentle, patient nature was a perfect foil for it.

Mrs. Reynolds and her aunt were engaged in a lively discussion, Mr. Gardiner trailing along being them with his hands clasped at his back. Elizabeth lingered for a moment as they left, having forgotten her, and stared at the portrait. An ache bloomed in her heart, born of what-ifs and a year's worth of frustrated thoughts regarding her mistakes. The desire to alternately forget him, or to renew the acquaintance and beg his pardon to start anew, plagued her. Girlish, childish fantasies.

Her hand lifted and she touched the edge of the picture frame with a sigh.

"Oh, Darcy. What a mess I have made of everything. Can you ever forgive me?"

She brought her fingers to her lips, pressed a kiss on her own tips, and gently touched the painting. How bitter was the taste of regret. At least it was a gentle bitterness, as time passed the sting healed.

"Forgiveness is always attainable, Miss Bennet."

Elizabeth froze, the deep, dark voice washing over her. Had she imagined it? But that was a foolish thought. She was standing here, in his home, in front of his portrait. She waited until she was certain the first blush of red had faded from her cheeks before she slowly turned to face him.

5

CHAPTER 2

He caught her pressing a kiss on his portrait. Fitzwilliam did not know what to make of it, but he admired the slow turn of her body as she faced him, expression composed. Her eyes were the same, clear and dark, mysterious as a winter lake. A faint tinge of pink was the only betrayal of her emotions. He did not mock her—how many times had he spoken to her in his mind? Taken her in his arms and brushed aside her worries, her distrust, and made everything the way he wished it to be through the indomitable force of his will?

In reality, one sometimes encountered a soul as formidable as one's own. He stood in front of such a soul, though it was housed in an infinitely more appealing exterior, hidden in the soft flesh and witty personage of Elizabeth Bennet.

"Are you well?" he asked, forgoing the usual pleasantries. He determined them unnecessary now, considering.

"Yes," she said, low contralto tones sending a tightening through his body. How would her voice sound in a different situation? "I am well. And yourself?" Her eyes searched his face. "You are in good health and spirits, I hope?"

"I am."

They fell silent and Fitzwilliam cursed himself. How ridiculous they both were, standing as if strangers when they both wanted the other. He wanted her and he knew she would not be standing here, unusually quiet, if she felt nothing. Would not have kissed him—his portrait—if she felt nothing. But . . .

"Why would you feel you need forgiveness?" he asked. "You have not wronged me."

She closed her eyes a moment, full mouth thinning, and then opened them again as if steeling herself. "I had hoped you would forget that question," she said in a wry tone and sighed. "We were told you were not in residence and would not return until to tomorrow, or else I would never have disturbed you. Please forgive me."

Fitzwilliam smiled, amused. "How neatly you sidestep my question. Well done. But I am not a fool, Miss Bennet." He allowed a hint of steel to creep into his tone. He would indulge her in much, but in this, he would have the truth. He required that truth. He needed to be certain if her feelings had changed since the previous April. If he had a chance with her. "Truth, Miss Bennet. You are not a coward."

She regarded him for a long moment, then lowered her eyes. "I am aware of what you did for my sister. You did not have to do it—I do not know why you did. But you have brought her great happiness and I must thank you as well as apologize. I misjudged you, and I have been sorry for it." Her eyes met his again. "And I do not thank you for forcing me to admit to such a thing. My pride is as great as your own."

"No doubt." He was silent another moment, choosing his words carefully. "We both have our pride, and we both made mistakes. I helped Charles and your sister because it was the right thing to do."

"This is not an attempt to—" she stopped, and he watched

7

in fascination as she blushed again. "I mean, I am not trying to renew any, oh, how vexing. Please excuse me, I really must rejoin my aunt and uncle, they will be missing me. They wandered on without me and now they must—"

He had heard enough. Fitzwilliam stepped forward and seized her hand, bringing it to his lips, his eyes claiming hers. "We have both suffered enough, Elizabeth."

She stopped speaking, falling silent except for the gentle exhalations of her breath as her lips parted in what he knew was an unconscious invitation. It ached, and something dark awakened in him. Not for the first time, but for the first time since he had last seen her. Or rather, since he had penned his letter to her, wrestling with savage thoughts and even more savage impulses. If this were a different time, and a different world, he could simply demand her in an act of Droit du seigneur, claim her as his own and be damned with the consequences. She felt for him, he was certain of it. She would love him, even if she did not now.

She had no choice but to love him, now that she had come to him willingly, and all but declared her feelings for him.

"I have waited for you to come to me," he murmured. "I told myself I would not disturb you and that I would leave you alone as long as you wished it. But you have come here, and you have asked for my forgiveness. That makes you mine, Miss Bennet."

"I—what are you saying, Mr. Darcy?"

She was flustered, one of the rare times he had seen her speechless in anything but anger. Fitzwilliam brushed his lips against her hand and watched as her eyelashes fluttered and her breath caught. A pulse jumped in the hollow of her neck and her chest rose. She was struggling as he struggled. Tamping down desire, fighting an impulse to allow the heart and not the mind to rule.

"I am saying," he replied very gently, "that this time I will not let you go."

He drew her into his arms, and giving her another few heartbeats to protest, lowered his head when she did not. And branded her as his.

~

He must be a sorcerer, or even a devil with the dark, piercing eyes which seized all her common sense and trampled it into the dust. His lips on hers set ablaze a heat she had thought ruthlessly crushed. After all, she was never to see him again, he would never be hers. Now with his arms crushing her to his chest and his lips demanding surrender, she realized the girlish dreams she had allowed herself at night just might come true. But when he said she was his . . . did he mean his wife or his mistress?

Thoughts fled under his sensual perusal. His hands did not wander, though his arms continued to tighten and the press of his body made it plain he desired her as she desired him.

"Elizabeth," he murmured against her mouth, the trailed a caress down the side of her neck. "You came to me."

"I . . .I did not mean to." She could not lie to him. She truly had not meant to see him. "But I suppose if you are happy to see me, then all is well."

He began to shake and she blinked. Laughter burst from his lips, a deep, masculine chuckle and she peered up at him but despite the amusement, his eyes were still burning.

"Do you have any idea how singular a woman you are, Elizabeth Bennet?"

She stiffened, about to retort, but paused and made herself forgo her usual instinct to bristle and defend herself. He had not meant to be insulting. He was simply infuriatingly arrogant. That was unlikely to change. Ever. Even on his deathbed.

"If you say so."

"I do say so." He stepped back, releasing her, and regarded her with an inscrutable stare, eyes narrowed. "I am giving a masquerade ball tomorrow evening. You would honor me with your presence.

Of all the things she had expected, an invitation to a ball had not been it. It threw her off. "I . . . I did not pack a suitable gown. I was not intending on attending such events while with my aunt and uncle."

"They are invited, too, of course," he replied, unperturbed. "Do not worry about your dress. I will see to it."

She drew herself up in a snap. "You certainly will not, Sir! I am not your—" she cut herself off, not wanting to say the indelicate word.

His brow hiked up, devilment in his eyes. "My mistress? No, you certainly are no mistress. However, since I was indelicate enough to extend such an invitation knowing you had no suitable attire, it is my responsibility to make amends. Of course, I would extend this offer to your Aunt as well."

Elizabeth's jaw clenched, then she sighed. "You are a devil. I could refuse for myself all day long, but I would not deny my lovely aunt such a treat."

He grinned at her, an unexpectedly boyish expression, but even as she blinked, it was gone, replaced by his more characteristic soberness. "No, indeed, I did not think you would refuse that. You cherish your family, after all."

She gave him a look. "Do not suppose I will always be caught so unwary for you to manipulate, sir."

"I do not suppose it at all, Miss Bennet. In fact, I rather look forward to the opposite."

The way he said it sent a shiver down her spine.

CHAPTER 3

Mr. Darcy escorted her to her aunt and uncle and when she thought he would politely take his leave, he instead astonished her when he paused to engage her uncle in amiable chatter, the kind of relaxed conversation one might have a familiar neighbor. Elizabeth stared at him as if he had grown two heads, wondering where this egalitarian, nearly charming man had come from. The one who would not dance in Meryton because he refused to be introduced to partners and did not enjoy dancing with strangers.

Though, of course, she reminded herself that that had not truly been the case, had it? For all his aura of cool control, there ran in him a reserved streak which prevented him from engaging in casual discourse with people he did not know. On any other man, she might have labeled the trait as shyness.

It only added to his appeal, of course. There was something alluring about a strong man with a vulnerable side to his nature. Alluring, and approachable, as if a mere mortal such as she could deign to touch the hem of his robe. Elizabeth smiled at her own fancies and he caught the look, for his eyes held hers for a long moment, a gleam of warmth obvious even to her relations, and certainly to Mrs. Reynolds, who nodded approvingly at Elizabeth.

"I will certainly take you up on the offer," her uncle replied heartily to Darcy's offer of the use of his lake for fishing. "I fear I must escort my ladies home, however, for my wife is beginning to look faint and I am not quite so young a man that I should be able to carry the fair damsel all the way to the carriage in my arms." Uncle grinned at his wife, who waved a hand and smiled.

"Away with you, Mr. Gardiner."

Darcy approached Elizabeth, lowering his head ever so slightly so his words would reach only her ears. "I will see you tomorrow evening, my dear. Do not try to flee me. I will be like Hades, and open the underworld to bring you back to my domain."

His voice was a deep caress, though his expression remained so entirely neutral no one would dare imagine he was whispering such scandalous nothings in her ear.

Elizabeth said nothing rather than embarrass herself with a stutter, and allowed him to hand her into the carriage, his fingers strong and warm around her hand. He released her with a subtle squeeze and caress of his thumb and her skin fair ached where he had touched her as they drove away.

"Such a charming young man," her aunt was saying. "Elizabeth, you told me he was cold and taciturn."

"I cannot fathom it, Aunt. This is the most relaxed I have ever seen him." She could not help another blush.

Her aunt and uncle exchanged a glance. "He escorted you from the gallery," Mrs. Gardiner said. "Did you have an opportunity to speak much?"

"Oh, yes, he assured me he was in no way put out by our presence," Elizabeth hurried to say. "And offered the invitation to the masquerade tomorrow evening and then to escort me back to you and uncle. He was nothing but courteous."

"Not proud at all," her uncle grunted. "I truly believe he meant the offer of the lake for fishing. I shall take him up on it, too, see if I do not."

Elizabeth could imagine nothing more pleasant than to sit on the grounds of Pemberley in front of the beautiful blue lake on a summer day with the warmth of the sun on the back of her neck. Nothing more pleasant, that was, than the warm breath of Pemberley's master on her neck. And on her lips, and his arms.—she tore her mind away from that train of thought lest her cheeks turn a betraying shade of red. Pink was enough of a betrayal.

"Well, what shall we have for lunch?" she asked, firmly turning the subject away from the confusing, haunting, irresistible master of Pemberley.

~

The next day went by in blur, Elizabeth desperately attempting to hold onto her calm and common sense and not think too much on Darcy. What his kiss meant, the meaning in his words. Had he made her an offer of some kind or was it merely a fashionable soft of flirtation a country miss like herself was not supposed to take seriously, only to enjoy and laugh off as what it was? Confusion was the least of her emotions, along with the feeling that by accepting a dress from Darcy, she would place herself in his power. As if by clothing her in satin and lace purchased by his own hand she someone, magically, became his. As if he truly could whisk her away to his underground castle and keep her prisoner to do his will.

Elizabeth shivered in broad daylight, though the sun was warm and the breeze fresh. There was no denying how strongly her physical reaction was to him. He had only to look at her with his dark eyes and she was caught in a snare until he chose to release her. If Darcy ever knew how much she thought on him, he would either think her completely foolish and avoid her entirely—which she was beginning to realize was not his desire, at all—or he would seek, like any man, to gain the upper hand and bring her under his power. Not that she thought him dishonorable. But clearly, he had a purpose in inviting her to his ball. He could have waited a day or two and sought out her company in a less public fashion, one that would not expose him to his peers. Of course, a masqued ball meant he could dally with her at will and no one would be the wiser of her identity.

Not that she would be allowing any dallying, per se. She may be able to help herself from attention, but she was not quite so much a moth to his flame. Did she dare hope for a renewal of the sentiments she had previously rejected? Perhaps. But if he thought she would become his mistress, or even engage in a heavy flirtation, she would put him to rights immediately, even if her heart broke a little.

This was what she continued to tell herself throughout the day, steeling her will against him In the late afternoon, boxes arrived at their inn, and a maid came to them as Elizabeth and her aunt sat in the common parlor, sipping tea. They had enjoyed a brisk walk about the town, and Elizabeth noted a number of carriages traveling on the main road that was a way to Pemberley.

"Parcels for you, Ma'am," the girl said, curtsying. Her eyes were alight with curiosity but she said nothing further. "I had them sent up to your rooms."

Aunt Gardiner rose. "Well, niece, shall we?" Despite her composed outward appearance, Elizabeth sensed an underlying eagerness in her aunt's manner and smiled.

They ascended the stairs and entered Elizabeth's room, where a stack of boxes was carefully placed on the bed.

The women exchanged a glance, making a tacit agreement to not appear too eager to open the offerings sent by Pemberley. Elizabeth opened a large rectangular box, a small card on top of the paper with her name written in elegant script. Pushing aside the wrapping, she inhaled, and silently lifted the gown up.

"How lovely," Aunt Gardiner said. "Such good taste."

The silk was a deep blush rose, a slightly deeper than pastel shade which she knew would bring a rosy hue to her skin and offset her dark hair. The trimmings on the gown were simple and elegant, nothing at all fussy. If Darcy had not chosen it, or at least given detailed instructions himself, she would be very much surprised. It reflected his own austere but impeccably tailored preference in dress.

Elizabeth carefully draped the gown across the bed and opened a second square box, revealing a gold half mask and white opera gloves. A third box slightly larger than her palm was next. Lifting the top, she could not help the gasp that escaped her lips.

"Oh," Aunt said. "Oh, my."

The necklace was exquisite, a tripled strand of delicate pearls with a gold cross pendant. There were matching earrings and a bracelet interspersed with winking diamonds.

"Niece . . ." Aunt Gardiner's voice was troubled. "He is rich as any lord, of course, but what would he send you such a bounty? Have you told me everything that was between you? This is more the sort of gift a man would send his future wife, or his—"

Aunt Gardiner stopped, but Elizabeth knew what word was in her mind. Mistress. Her fingers trolled every so slightly as she picked up the necklace. "I think he is simply rich as any Lord and, perhaps, eager to make amends for our previous quarrel."

"This time I will not let you go,." he had said.

Elizabeth had been trying to convince herself that those words had meant nothing. It was better to steel herself for disappointment, guard her heart to avoid seeing intentions where none were present. Better to remain cordial and slightly distant, despite the heated promise of his kiss.

She could not help but realize she had to be fooling herself. The question was what kind of fooling was it? Either he desired her for a wife or mistress, an insult to her character she would never accept, or he was flirting.

Either way, Elizabeth had the feeling she would find out at the ball. The one surety she could count on with Mr. Darcy, was that he would make his desires unmistakably known, and in his own time.

CHAPTER 4

However, after giving the matter some thought, she returned the jewelry box to Pemberley with a note.

I thank you for the loan of the gown, Mr. Darcy, it is very fine and much appreciated. However, I cannot accept the pearls no matter how lovely they are. I feel our limited acquaintance does not warrant so personal a gift, though once again, I thank you for thinking of me. My aunt is also very pleased with the gown sent for her, and declares you to be the kindest gentleman in Derbyshire.

E.B.

The matter of propriety resolved, Elizabeth turned her attention to writing her letters for the week, whiling away the time until the hour came to make ready. Aunt Gardiner would perform Jane's office and assist with her hair; Elizabeth likewise would help her aunt.

A light tap on the door brought her away from her letters. "Yes?"

The door opened, maid bobbing a quick curtsy. "Ma'am, a gentleman in the parlor to see you."

Elizabeth rose. "I will be down presently." The maid had stressed the word gentleman, so that eliminated the possibility that the man in question as a servant or messenger. There was really only one other person it could be, but why in the world would Darcy call on her? Did he not have a ball to ready for and guests to greet?

After tidying her appearance, Elizabeth descended the stairs and entered the parlor. "Mr. Darcy."

He turned, the expression on his face edged with displeasure. "Miss Bennet. When I give a woman a gift, I do not expect for it to be returned."

Mr. Darcy nodded towards a round side table, and on the top sat the jewelry box. She stared at it and then him. "You could have sent a servant."

"No, I could not have, for I am aware of the stubbornness of your nature and I have not the time today to entertain your stubbornness."

He moved to the table, picked up the box, and crossed the room, handing it to her. "This is yours. Pray accept it in the spirit in which it was given."

"The bullying sort?"

His eyes narrowed, and he chuckled. "Nothing is ever easy with you, is it? At least I shall never be bored. Miss Bennet—Elizabeth." He closed the final distance between them and looked down at her, voice a caress. "It is my desire these pearls know the warmth of touching your skin, as it is a right I know you are not yet ready to grant me."

Her eyes widened. The nature of his words left little to the imagination, an allusion to the stolen kiss, a desire for another. But he could not think so little of her that he believed she would allow him the intimacy of a husband or at least, a betrothed?

She took a deep breath, steadying her pounding heart. "I fear I may have given you the wrong impression, Sir, and I realize now I must refuse to attend the ball."

He stilled, watching her with the unblinking intensity of a hunter. She moved away a step, attempting to break the draw of his body, so near her own.

"I do not have the sophistication to indulge in a flirtation of the kind I am told the worldly ladies and gentlemen of London often do, and I cannot allow you to believe I would ever . . ." Her voice faltered, because she knew once she denied him forever, she would never see him again. But so be it. "I cannot be your mistress. I am not saying that is what you had in mind, or even that you would deign to ask, but I am a simple woman and unversed in these sorts of games. I do not know how to judge your behavior."

She firmed her mouth to avoid allowing him to see her tremble as she looked away. Humiliation curled in her breast, for she had admitted her ignorance as well as, perhaps, made a laughable presumption.

"Is that why you believe I want, Elizabeth?" he asked, voice soft. "To have you as my mistress?"

She said nothing. What could she say? She had already laid herself bare. At least she had not suffered the ultimate indignation and admitted her love for him only to have him scorn her. At least that final secret she might keep hidden in her heart.

"I do not want you for my mistress," he said. "Here."

Confused, she glanced at him, staring at the box he held out. "I do not understand."

"I expect to see you at the ball tonight, Elizabeth. If I do not, I will be forced to fetch you, and then I will be in a poor mood."

She took the box, starting when his free hand brushed her cheek. "I—"

"You do not think much of my honor, do you?"

"I never thought you to be dishonorable."

His eyes were enigmatic, and he smiled a little. "Good. I will take my leave so you may ready yourself. Not even five minutes late, Elizabeth. Do you understand?"

Warmth spread in her chest, mingling with irritation over his commanding nature. "I will consider it, Sir." But her arch tone conveyed her acceptance.

Darcy bowed and with a final, heated look which would have her begging for kisses in another moment, he took his leave and Elizabeth returned to her room.

With those mixed feelings, she prepared for the ball. When it came time to don her jewelry, she hesitated, but took the box out from underneath her pillow, slowly draping the strands around her neck. The cross settled in the hollow of her neck, and she could not help but feel as if the necklace was a mark. But of what? Having played their conversation over and over in her mind, she was certain they indicated a desire to renew his previous offer of marriage. He did not say it outright, but considering their history, it was understandable he would proceed with greater caution this time around. Once he was certain of her response, he would ask for her hand.

Armed with a new resolution that nothing should spoil the budding understanding between them, Elizabeth knocked on her aunt's door.

～

Aunt Gardiner's eyes grazed Elizabeth's neck several times on the way to Pemberley, but she said nothing. Elizabeth was grateful, for she needed time to decipher exactly where she and Darcy stood before attempting to explain to her aunt that everything was well. Everything would not be well until he asked her to be his wife. Already, the intimate behavior between them—the use of her Christian name where others might hear, the extravagant gift of jewelry, not to mention the kiss—were all enough to compromise her if anyone had ever witnessed the interactions. However, his denial of wanting her for a mistress alone with his continued use of her first name gave her hope.

No, Darcy was not a dishonorable man. He would know that any young lady of genteel birth would take his signals to be an unspoken matrimonial intention. And he was not a man to play games with a woman's heart or reputation.

The carriage pulled up to the grand entrance of Pemberley and a footman in white gloves and impeccable sober livery assisted the ladies out, speaking a polite welcome in a polished voice. It was another point in Darcy's favor, the elegance of his staff.

The ballroom, transformed from the day of their visit, was lit with a warm glow. Couples mingled, dressed in the most elegant of attire. Elizabeth was secure behind her mask and grateful for the dress Darcy sent her, for she was as well-clad as any lady here, if not dressed even finer than some. A man detached himself from the crowd, a lady with light brown hair and a gown the color of the summer sky on his arm. She would recognize him anywhere, of course. The deliberate stride and intense, focused stare. But the beauty of the woman, hidden by the mask, momentarily derailed her admiration of Darcy.

Darcy bowed, the woman on his arm making a curtsy. "Miss Bennet, Mr. and Mrs. Gardiner, may I introduce my sister, Georgiana?"

His sister! Of course. Elizabeth returned the curtsy, feeling foolish though she hoped none of it showed in her face. Smiling, she said, "It is a pleasure to meet you, Miss Georgiana. I have been regaled with tales of your charm and accomplishments."

The woman laughed. "By my brother, no doubt. It is wonderful to meet you as well, Miss Elizabeth, for I have heard many pleasing things of you as well."

The light smile turned mischievous and Elizabeth blinked, glancing at Darcy. "I would be shocked to hear it."

"We will have to speak soon," Georgiana replied. Glancing at her brother, "As Miss Elizabeth is now arrived, shall we open the ball?"

Had he been waiting for her? Elizabeth's realized that if Georgiana was under the impression the opening of the ball was waiting on her arrival, then Darcy must have told her what for.

"I informed my sister you were threatening not to attend unless I promised to ask for no more than two dances," Darcy said.

"Two dances?" Aunt Gardiner exclaimed. "That will be a very pretty sight, indeed, for you both have a natural elegance of form."

"I can think of no reason why I would deny you, Sir," Elizabeth managed to say, "as I know you are not a man given to stepping on toes."

"Your feet," he said, "are safe from me. It is all I can promise."

As his eyes held hers, she once again was aware of a meaning underneath his words.

"I will hold you to such a promise," she replied.

He and Georgiana took their leave to open the ball, and as they walked to the center of the dance floor, her aunt came close in order to speak to Elizabeth softly. "Niece? I think there is something you are not telling me. Two dances? And after the gifts, I cannot continue to think it a coincidence. Has he made his intentions to you known?"

"I believe the matter will be resolved soon, Aunt."

"Good." Her expression was worried. "If your name was linked with Mr. Darcy's in a certain manner, and there was no engagement—you do know you would be ruined, Elizabeth? Please be careful. Powerful men often take what they want and disregard the consequences, and pursuing any legal redress would be costly for our family in more than one way."

"I understand. Please, do not worry. I do not intend to allow him to place me in an unfortunate situation." No matter how much she yearned for his kiss, or for the heat in his eyes to manifest in a way that should be reserved for the marriage bed.

CHAPTER 5

Darcy was discreet. He did not claim her for a dance until he had danced with several other ladies and Elizabeth with other gentlemen. She watched him covertly. He also danced with his sister, and with a tall, thin woman Elizabeth realized was Caroline Bingley. She had not known her sister-in-law would be present, and was grateful for the masks. Caroline had never liked her, and her cutting wit at Elizabeth's expense had only increased after Jane had wed Charles. Elizabeth was convinced Caroline would never be pleased her brother was happy, for Jane was not a fashionable heiress, but merely a beautiful country gentleman's daughter.

Elizabeth took a break between sets to fetch herself a drink, and ascertain her aunt and uncle were enjoying themselves. Once Mr. Gardiner was ensconced in the card room and her aunt had made the acquaintance of an older lady, and they were happily conversing and benevolently watching the younger dancers.

"Go, enjoy your evening, my dear," her aunt said, waving a hand. "I am quite able to look after myself."

Elizabeth did as she was bid and it was not a few moments later that Darcy appeared at her elbow. She stared, and nearly sloshed her wine for he had emerged unexpectedly from a shift in the crowd.

"Darcy! You startled me."

"My apologies." He took her glass and handed it to passing servant, then clasped her hand. "Come. It is time."

"You make it sound as if we are heading to a sacrificial bonfire, Sir, and not a dance."

His lips quirked at her teasing. "If there is such a bonfire, then tonight our patron must be Dionysus, and you would be the maiden laid upon the altar of his desire."

"Poor maiden," she murmured. "Such a fate."

Behind his austere mask, eyes glinted. "A maidenly state can be altered, madam. Then you would escape his clutches."

She stared up at him. "But not the clutches of the man altering my state."

He drew her closer, too close, as if the throng of people was a shroud for them. "Do you not desire to change your state?"

"I desire many things, Mr. Darcy, not the least of which is to avoid throwing myself upon an altar as a sacrifice to lust."

He smiled and drew her along to the dance. The first set they did not speak, but when he could, he held her eyes, and every touch of his hand made clear his feelings. Frustration grew. He was behaving like a man bent on seduction, and certain of his lady's cooperation. But had she not told him she would not be seduced?

"Something disturbs you," he said when the first set was over. He watched her carefully, having retreated behind his customary restraint, as if sensing her agitation.

Elizabeth took a deep breath, struggled with her course of action. She could confront him, but that would only make her look like a fool and a shrew. She did enjoy his attentions, and she knew where her line was drawn. Perhaps she should simply revel in his warmth and when it was time, if her hopes were not rewarded, make a gentle farewell. It was not as if she did not have a home to return to, her sojourn here was meant to be brief.

"I am fine," she said finally, lowering her eyes.

His hand caught her chin, lifting her face up. She gasped and stepped away. "Darcy!"

"Forgive me. Perhaps I am—" He paused, expression inscrutable, then shook his head against whatever words he was about to speak. "Come. Dance with me again."

"But. . ."

His expression warmed. "Be bold, Elizabeth, and trust me."

Trust. . .she bit her lip, but accepted his hand because if this was all she was to have of him, so be it. At least she would have one magical, masqued night to remember him by when she left.

~

"Why, it is Elizabeth Bennet!"

Elizabeth stiffened but turned to greet Caroline Bingley. She would recognize the light, mocking voice anywhere. Caroline approached, two other ladies with her.

"Miss Bingley," she greeted.

"Fancy seeing you here, I could not countenance it at first, but then I was certain of it when I saw the look upon Darcy's face." She laughed lightly, and leaned in, lowering her voice with a mischievous smile as if begging a confidence. "Tell me truly, how did you manage an invitation? Darcy never forgives a person who has slighted him."

"Perhaps," she said in her most icy voice, "he is a better man than you give him credit for."

Caroline laughed, and pulled away, glancing at her companions. "This is Elizabeth Bennet, the sister of my brother's wife. Jane. A lovely girl from the country, sweet and such good sense to have snapped up my brother."

Elizabeth smiled, the expression edged. "You make her sound rather mercenary, Miss Bingley. It was a match born of love."

"Oh, I daresay. He loved her beauty and she his money, but that is how these things go, is it not? Such a sweet girl, in any case."

Her companions laughed and Elizabeth drew herself up, enraged. She hid it behind code courtesy. "Are you yet unbetrothed, Miss Bingley? It seems as if beauty in a woman is no guarantees of an advantageous match, after all, even if she is not poor as my sister was."

Caroline's face whitened and she inhaled abruptly. "It seems, after having danced two sets in a row with Darcy, that you are taking lessons from Jane." She smiled. "I have never seen him bestow such attention on a partner but, after all, we women must do what we can to make our way in this world even if it is only as a rich man's mistress."

Elizabeth's head snapped back as if she had been slapped. She did not know what she had done to deserve this malice. The shocked silence of the ladies at her side proclaimed Caroline's words had indeed gone beyond the bounds of propriety, even among a set that used words as if they were weapons.

"Miss Bennet."

Elizabeth turned, looking up into Darcy's face. She was angry, so angry, but she would not descend to Caroline Bingley's wine fueled behavior.

"I believe your aunt is searching for you," he said, and looked over Elizabeth's shoulder. She would have taken a step back, for the look in his eyes, aimed at the woman now at her back, was not pleasant. "Miss Bingley. Perhaps some fresh air would do you good. You seem overwrought."

Elizabeth walked away, pushing through the crowd to search for her aunt, so angry she bumped into at least two people, though she made hurried apologies.

"Elizabeth." A hand on her elbow, taking over her steps and steering her into a quiet corner. "I heard some of what she said. Do not let her trouble you. She has difficulties of her own she is dealing with. Poorly, it seems."

She shook her head, took a deep breath. "I am not troubled. But perhaps it is time I left, I seem to have the start of a headache."

"You will do no such thing," was his crisp reply. "Come. Somewhere quiet and a drink to settle your nerves—"

"Nerves!"

"Ah. A poor choice of words, perhaps. But come."

She allowed him to lead her through the crowd. "My aunt was not looking for me was she?"

"No. She is quite happily engaged in conversation and I believe was recently persuaded to dance."

They left the ballroom. "Where are you taking me?"

"My study. No one will disturb you there and you may sit in front of the fire as long as you like."

It was an intimate gesture, though he had firmly leashed the tendrils of seduction in his former manner. Now he was brisk, nearly solicitous, and Elizabeth relaxed.

Entering his study, she glanced around. The only light was the fire, which was well underway. "I had the servants keep it fed for I feared I would need a moment or two of quiet myself before the evening was over," Darcy said. "You might not believe it, but I do not truly enjoy balls. My sister loves them, however."

"I believe it." The first time they had met had been at a dance, and he had done nothing but stand in a corner and scowl at everyone.

Darcy settled her into a large, comfortable armchair in front of the fire, then returned moments later with a glass.

"It is what I drink," he said, somewhat apologetic, "but Georgiana sneaks sips when she thinks I am not paying attention."

She took the offered spirit and downed it in one gulp. His brow rose in surprise and she nearly smiled at him. There were things he did not know about Elizabeth Bennet, such as she liked her port just as much as any man.

After a pause, he said, "There. All better."

Elizabeth snorted, handing him the glass which he refilled. "It is not all better. That harridan implied—" she cut herself off, blushing. "It is bad enough she insults Jane, whom has never harmed a fly in her life, but to insinuate that I am attempting to . . . I will not even repeat the words."

"Hmm." He stood next to her, amusement on his face. At some point he had removed his mask, and reached down to pluck at the strings of hers so it fell in her lap. "Forget Caroline. You and I know the truth, and that is all that matters."

Elizabeth rose, facing him. "I do not know the truth, Darcy. Or rather, I know that you desire me." The drink was making her bold, stripping away the usual care she took with her speech. "Though you have said you will not make me your mistress?"

He stared at her, gaze steady. "You keep mentioning the word mistress. I am beginning to think that is your desire, though it is not mine."

Her eyes narrowed. "Now you do insult me. Very well, I shall take my leave."

He caught her around the waist, forestalling her steps. "One moment, Elizabeth. You have accused me and I find I am no longer willing to endure your accusations without defending myself. But if you think so poorly of me, then I may as well indulge."

CHAPTER 6

His head swooped down, lips claiming hers in an angry kiss. Angry and frustrated. Darcy drew her flush along his body, arms locking her into place. Struggle was the last thing on her mind, the sensual onslaught overwhelming all of her good sense and even a good portion of her ire. Her entire body sighed, and Elizabeth realized, dimly, the true source of her agitation. She wanted him. She craved him and her continued denial of what she desired had been eating away at her. The thought of never seeing him again had been eating at her. Two instincts warred, dignity versus desire. Her pride against her passion.

She gasped against his lips, feeling the hardness of his body pressing against her. His laugh was short, hollow. A hand rose, gripping the back of her neck.

"You want me as much as I want you," he said in a low, nearly savage tone. His free thumb caressed her lips, and she arched against him involuntarily.

"I always wanted you," she said in an agonized tone. "Even though I should not. Even though you will be the ruin of me."

"You are the only one who believes I will be your ruin, Elizabeth." He cursed, a short, harsh word. "Do you think I am made of stone? What do you think it would do to me to hear a second refusal?"

She stared up at him, shocked. "What?"

His smile was grim, and mocking. But the mockery was aimed at himself. "I never know the thoughts behind your eyes. You are the only woman I cannot read, even my sister is an open book to me and she is as sensible a female as any I have ever met. Do you know how many times I have had to stop myself from overwhelming you with my desire, seducing from you the words I craved to hear?"

"What words? All you have ever spoken of was desire."

"It was easier. In that, at least, I know we are of one accord."

His hand slid up her body, cupping a breast as he watched her face. The sudden caress shocked her, but strong fingers slid inside her bodice and somehow, even through the corset he was able to touch her. She moaned and he closed his eyes as if in pain.

"I want you," he said. "I will have you. But not as my mistress, Elizabeth. As my wife. If you tell me no, then I will leave you as much as it pains me to do so. Do you understand me?" His hands tangled in her hair, as if in emphasis. "If you do not promise to marry me, Elizabeth, I will not give you the touch you crave."

His head lowered, lips brushing the side of her neck. "I know what you crave. I can ease you. Say you will marry me."

She uttered a choked laugh. "As if you have to ask! I have agonized since we kissed in the gallery over whether you desired me only for your mistress or if you would offer again. I did not dare speak."

"Elizabeth." His hand in her hair hadn't gentled, his voice softening.

"I treated you unfairly, and I could not imagine you still cared for me."

His lips grazed her jaw. "Of course I care. I am only a man, my love, with a man's fragile ego."

He said the last words with a thread of dark humor in his tone. She peered up at him with a tumbling smile and he sucked in a breath.

"I should do the honorable thing and push you away from me, but I cannot. You will be my wife, as soon as I can arrange it."

She knew what he was asking. Ardor had not cooled as they spoke, only deepened. She wrapped her arms around his neck. "I do not wish to be parted from you."

The simple words spurred him into action. He lifted her, striding to the desk, the surface surprisingly clear, but then it was Darcy. He would not tolerate disorder.

"What are you—"

"Hush." He pushed her onto the table, gentle but implacable, eyes burning. "Just feel, Elizabeth. There is more than one benefit to being my wife."

She could barely utter an exclamation as he lifted her skirts, pushing cloth over her thighs, exposing the delicate undergarments covering her legs. His hand cupped her flesh, bared by a dainty slit and she moaned. He pressed, and soon his fingers toyed with her, eliciting a startling physical sensation she instinctively understood her aching body had been craving.

Elizabeth closed her eyes, giving herself up to his sorcery, and stiffened when she felt the touch of lips, and then tongue.

"Darcy!"

Strong hands held her wrists to the desk, his only response as he continued to kiss her womanhood. Her thighs parted further, of their own accord, and a haze of pleasure overcame her.

Elizabeth cried out, straining against his hold, and the warm breath of his laughter tickled flesh. There was a release, but also . . . her hips squirmed. Nearing a feeling of desperation she said,

"More. I—I do not know what is wrong with me. I need more."

Darcy rose and the shadows the firelight cast over his face would have frightened her if she did not trust him completely.

"Are you certain, Elizabeth?"

She instinctively knew what he must be asking her and she nodded. He contemplated her, head tilted.

"I find," he said slowly, "that I am not so honorable as I thought. I should tell you no, and wait for our marriage bed. But I cannot. I want to see you. Taste you."

He drew her off the desk and began to do the office of a lady's maid, undressing her with swift, certain motions.

"Take you."

Her gown puddled to the floor, and Elizabeth's brow furrowed as she wondered where he had learned to so expertly deal with a lady's corset and undergarments. The slightly peevish thoughts distracted her momentarily from the fact that he was stripping her naked and she was letting him. Wanting him.

There was no shyness as she stood before him in nothing but the cross around her neck and as she looked down at her body, realized the nipples of her breasts were hardened into tiny buds. Darcy lowered his head, taking one in his mouth and she cried out, back arching as he taught her yet another unknown purpose of her flesh.

Palming the other, he kneaded her flesh. She lifted a leg, wrapping it around his waist without any conscious thought, the place between her thighs aching, pulsing. Hesitantly, her hand slid down his chest. She had observed the horses mate, and her mother had once stammered a bumbling explanation. She understood, in thereby, how the practice went.

He hissed as her hand found him, brushing a steel hard length. Darcy lifted her back onto the desk and lying beneath him, the firelight on her skin, completely vulnerable to his perusal, she did, indeed, feel like a sacrificial maiden. Only her Dionysus was standing over her.

He freed himself, never taking eyes from hers, and when she glanced down to observe the engorged length of him, her eyes widened.

He must have seen the flash of panic. "Trust me, Elizabeth. Your body was made for mine."

She trusted him. His hands were on her ankles as he spread her legs, draping her thighs over his shoulders as his member nudged her entrance. He slid inside and it was so tight, the intimacy nearly unbearable. There was no separation between his flesh and hers and as he continued to push inside her, her body gave way until he was seated fully.

"And now," he said, and withdrew and entered her again. And again. And again.

Elizabeth clutched the sides of the desk as he took her, strokes forceful, the sensation in her body wringing a shuddering cry from her throat. With each stroke, a sharp, relentless pleasure until for the second time, he taught her the advantage of being his wife.

He withdrew from her body and she saw he was still hard, body unrelieved. "I did not wait so long to finish so quickly," he said, interpreting her look.

He lifted her off the desk and into his arms, striding back to the armchair in front of the fire. Her feet touched the floor and she stared at him, confused. He stared, taking her hands.

"Straddle me, Elizabeth."

"You want me to . . . cover you?" Like a stallion with a mare. His body, glistening with the wetness she had felt between her thighs, stood at attention. Licking her lips, Elizabeth placed her knees on either side of his and grasped him, guiding him towards her entrance.

His hands clasped her waist as he urged her down, spearing her from below. She moaned, head tilting back and his hands were on her breasts, playfully slapping her flesh as she moved on him, his hips undulating. Fingers touched the other spot between her thighs and her body roared back to life, even though she had thought herself exhausted.

"I am the only man who will ever see you thus, touch you thus." His voice was deep, guttural, his touch possessive. "The only man who will ever hear you scream your pleasure. And this is just the beginning, my Elizabeth."

He grabbed her hips, holding her still as she cried out, emptying inside her. Elizabeth collapsed on his chest, her entire body wracked in trembles, and his hands roved up and down her back in soft, soothing strokes.

They could not remain there all night. He kissed her neck. "My Elizabeth. I do not want to share you with anyone tonight, but we must return. We will get this ball over with and in the morning I will send for a special license and we will be wed soon. Very soon."

"Do I have to return to my aunt and uncle?" The words were ridiculous, she knew. Of course she could not stay with him. But her heart clenched at the thought of the separation.

He laughed softly. "I do not want to leave you either. I will invite your uncle to fish, and we'll sneak away for a few moments. Like illicit lovers, until we are married."

Darcy helped her redress, exiting the study for several moments and returning with a cloth and a pitcher of water. He cleaned her, the task as intimate as their lovemaking, and in the course of the cleansing they nearly succumbed again. He hurriedly helped her into her corset and gown, muttering curses under his breath the entire time as she attempted to right her hair.

"I hate balls," he said. "I would rather take you to my room and chain you to my bed."

Elizabeth smiled. "What about dinner?" she teased. "And your sister is certainly to come looking for you, and my aunt for me."

He sighed, and as soon as she was presentable they left the study, Elizabeth giggling like a schoolgirl and a reluctant smile on Darcy's face. As they approached the hall leading to the ballroom, his impassive public mask slowly descended, and she regretted its necessity. He paused, offering his arm formally.

"Well, Miss Elizabeth, shall we?"

~

The remainder of the evening passed in a blur. Mr. Darcy did not leave her side, except at dinner where he stared at her down the line of the table, making no attempt to conceal his attention. Talk inevitably ensued though in a subdued manner because this was Pemberley, and its master, after all.

"Quite a spectacle," she overheard a chill female voice say, and decided to ignore Caroline Bingley. "It is evident she has been successful in her mission. Do you know they disappeared at the same time for over an hour? A walk in the gardens, I daresay."

"Elizabeth," her aunt said, forehead creased, taking her

arm as they entered their carriage. Elizabeth's eyes flickered to her uncle who settled himself, hands draped over his belly, and began snore.

"All is well, Aunt," she whispered, taking the elder lady's hand. "In the morning, you shall see."

Because she was sane, she worried. A little. Not that she did not trust Mr. Darcy, but alone in her cold bed at night, she could not help but think it all a dream. She managed to sleep a little, mostly because the wine insisted, but she woke early in the morning and dressed, taking care with her appearance so she should not look as if she had spent a night in revelry. Nothing could be done for the faint circles under her eyes and she would not stoop to powders or creams. Refusing to brood in her room, she decided on a walk in the sunshine. It would add color to her cheeks and she would not feel quite so pathetic, as if she were a damsel in a tower awaiting her knight's pleasure.

Elizabeth strolled the town, pausing at the door of a baker's shop to inhale the scents wafting out when the sound of horses hooves interrupted her reverie. She turned, looking for the rider, and met Mr. Darcy's half amused, half annoyed, eyes.

"They told me you left on a walk," he said, dismounting. "Elizabeth, why did you not wait for me?"

"I was restless, and I did not know what time you would come."

He watched her face carefully and must have heard the hesitance in her voice for his expression darkened. "You did not think I would come."

His words were an accusation. She shrugged. "It is the fear of every lady, I think. That she gives her heart and her body and. . .but no. I knew you would come." The last words were said firmly, for she told herself to stop being foolish.

Mr. Darcy's expression softened, and he bowed, then

took her hand and drew her along. "Come. Your father is not here, so I will pay my respects to your uncle. And then I daresay you will have letters to write."

∾

"Engaged," her uncle said, astonished. He stared at Elizabeth and Mr. Darcy, nonplussed. "This is very sudden, but on behalf of the lady's father, let me offer most sincere congratulations!"

The men chattered, and Aunt Gardiner took her aside, relief on her face. "I am so happy for you, my dear, and after the way your two snuck away last night. . ."

Elizabeth's eyes widened. "You noticed?"

"Of course. You do not get to be my age without an understanding of the little tricks young people play. The wedding will be soon, yes?" Her eyes drifted to Elizabeth's middle.

Her bridegroom, of course, heard and turned. "It will be as soon as I arrange the special license. And we will have a celebration when the Bennet family arrives to mark the occasion."

He smiled at Elizabeth and took her hand again, drawing her close. She stared up into his eyes. "That sounds perfect."

His thumb brushed her cheek, and he lowered his head to speak quietly in her ear. "Soon, my love."

Uncle Gardiner cleared his throat. "My dear, why not give the young couple a few minutes alone? Remember how we were at that age."

Aunt giggled, and they left the parlour.

"Will you be unhappy that your elder sister does not attend the ceremony? I desire us to be wed straight away, in case of. . .family complications."

39

She took his meaning immediately, and a blush suffused her cheeks.

"No, Jane will understand. I am the happiest woman to wed the man I love."

He cupped her cheek. "And never doubt, Elizabeth, that I am the happiest man."

JOIN THE NEWSLETTER

New Release announcements,
giveaways,
ARC opportunities,
flash sales.

smarturl.it/coraaston

JOIN

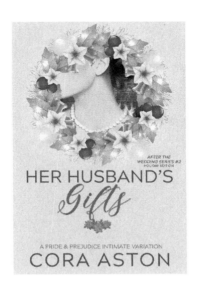

A childish prank forced them to marry. Now, Elizabeth and Darcy must make the most of their union, only Lizzy is convinced her husband could never love her.

Is convinced that it is really Anne, the daughter of Lady Catherine de Bourgh, whom he loves.

But with the holiday season comes a chance to truly begin their marriage…if only they can escape the machinations of those with ulterior motives…and if Darcy and Elizabeth can finally admit to each other the depths of their affection.

Her Husband's Gift is the second passionate short story in the **After the Wedding Series**, vignettes reimagining what may have happened with Mr. Darcy and Elizabeth at Pemberley after they married. These stories will not necessarily be told in chronological order or even feature the exact same Darcy & Elizabeth. Each short will include a tastefully written steamy sensual scene which enhances the exploration of marital intimacy between ODC. The author will make sweet versions available on her website. If you crave tales depicting the passion, angst, and temper of ODC as they navigate tumultuous but loving marriage, you will enjoy the After the Wedding shorts.

Download now for an emotional, romantic tale of the passions and struggles of marriage.

ABOUT THE AUTHOR

I suppose I should talk about myself in the third person, but I'm not going to. (Smile.) I'm a wife, a mother of four, and a lifelong tinkerer. I've dabbled in many different crafts and hobbies including jewelry making, baking, sewing, drawing.... And, of course, I am a lifetime avid reader of romance.

Escaping into the 'simpler' time of Jane Austen when gentlemen were required to court a lady with marriage in mind, and we didn't have to wheedle our daughter's into ditching the ripped black goth jeans in favor of a skirt....sigh. Bliss, right?

I've also always loved to write, and now I am combining two of my joys and hoping to share them with you. Like everything worth doing, this is a journey, and I'm happy to share it with you.

http://www.longbournlibrary.com/category/authors/cora-aston/

authorcoraaston@gmail.com

Printed in Great Britain
by Amazon